CH00799108

The Fly

a play

by

WALTER WYKES

WITHDRAWN

Black Box Press
Arlington, TX

Copyright © 2010 by Black Box Press

All rights reserved.

CAUTION: Professionals and amateurs are hereby warned that *The Fly* is subject to a royalty. It is fully protected under the copyright laws of the United States of America, and of all countries covered by the International Copyright Union (including the Dominion of Canada and the rest of the British Commonwealth), and of all countries covered by the Pan-American Copyright convention and the Universal Copyright Convention, and of all countries with which the United States has reciprocal copyright relations. All rights, including professional and amateur stage performing, motion picture, recitation, lecturing, public reading, radio broadcasting, television, video or sound taping, all other forms of mechanical or electronic reproduction, such as information storage and retrieval systems and photocopying, and the rights of translation into foreign languages, are strictly reserved.

Inquiries concerning all rights for *The Fly* should be directed to the playwright at: sandmaster@aol.com

ISBN 978-0-557-41422-2

First Edition

WITHDRAWN

WOODHOUSE COLLEGE LIBRARY	
RECEIVED	NUMBER
07/2012	R322 91 F
LOCATION	Class
TH	822.914 WYK

SCENE I

*[A half-lit bar. Early evening. A middle-aged man sits
nursing his drink, staring up at a silent television that flashes
mutely in the semi-darkness. A woman enters and watches for
a moment—then approaches and tosses her purse on the bar.]*

MURRAY

You came back.

EMMA

Uh-huh.

MURRAY

I was hoping you would.

EMMA

Were you?

MURRAY

Yeah.

EMMA

You don't know what you're getting into.
[He looks her over as she lights a cigarette.]
Buy me another drink?

MURRAY

Would. If I could. But I can't.

EMMA

So you won't?

MURRAY

No bartender.

EMMA

What—another smoke break?

MURRAY

Hell if I know.

EMMA

That guy is lung cancer waiting to happen.

MURRAY

Look who's talking.

EMMA

You've got me there.
        [She smiles. Takes another drag.]

MURRAY

I'm working on liver cancer myself.

EMMA

Always a good one.

MURRAY

He's not making it easy. Keeps disappearing. Still hasn't said two
words.

EMMA

It's kind of spooky—the way he just stares.

MURRAY

Maybe his larynx is shot.

EMMA

Maybe.

MURRAY

Maybe he's only got a few weeks to live. He knows the cancer's got
him, but he wants to give it the finger, so to speak, go out with the
smoke still in his lungs.

                    EMMA
Maybe he's already dead.

                    MURRAY
Could be.

                    EMMA
Bartending from beyond the grave.

                    MURRAY
You never know.

                    EMMA
I've seen horror films. I know how it starts. Half-empty bar. Two
strangers trying to have a pleasant conversation. People start
disappearing. No service. Next thing you know they're banging on
the window with severed limbs.

                    MURRAY
You make it sound so pleasant—being trapped in a horror film with
me.
     [She studies him.]

                    EMMA
I knew you wanted me, I could feel it—you called me here.

                    MURRAY
Did I?

                    EMMA
I've felt it once before.

                    MURRAY
Have you?

                    EMMA
That pull.

MURRAY

With someone else, you mean?

EMMA

He just ... sucked me in. Like gravity, you know. Like planets. It was inevitable. He was the spider. I was the fly.

MURRAY

Lucky guy.

EMMA

Maybe. I'm more trouble than I'm worth.
        [Pause.]

MURRAY

So why'd you leave? Just now. If I'm the spider and you're the fly ... why duck out?

EMMA

I had to make a call.

MURRAY

"A call."
        [She nods.]
That's very mysterious.
        [Pause.]
What kind of call?

EMMA

The personal kind.
        [Pause. MURRAY finishes his drink and hops over the bar.]
What are you doing?

MURRAY

You want a drink—right?

                    EMMA
[Laughs.]
What if he comes back?

                    MURRAY
I haven't seen the guy for over an hour. If he comes back now, I've
got really bad fucking luck. What do you want?

                    EMMA
Surprise me.

                    MURRAY
All right.
        [He mixes two drinks. She watches for a moment.]

                    EMMA
You know … you're just like them.

                    MURRAY
Like who?

                    EMMA
Your characters.
        [MURRAY stops.]

                    MURRAY
What?

                    EMMA
Your characters. In your books. You have that same sort of … I
don't know … reckless swagger, I guess. It's like—

                    MURRAY
Fuck.

                              EMMA

What?
        [Pause.]
What's wrong?

                              MURRAY

Nothing.
        [Pause.]
You know who I am?

                              EMMA

Sure.
        [Pause.]

                              MURRAY

How long?

                              EMMA

How long have I known? Right away. I recognized you as soon as—

                              MURRAY

Goddammit.

                              EMMA

What's the big deal?

                              MURRAY

I was hoping you didn't, that's all. It doesn't matter. I mean, if that's
why you're here, you're wasting your time, so …

                              EMMA

If that's why I'm here?

                              MURRAY

Right.

                              EMMA

I thought we'd already established why I was here.

MURRAY

Look. Who did you call before?

EMMA

I'm sorry?

MURRAY

When you left? Who did you call?

EMMA

None of your business.

MURRAY

Give me your phone.

EMMA

What?

MURRAY

Your cell phone. Give it here.

EMMA

I don't think so.

MURRAY

Right now.

EMMA

Are you serious?

MURRAY

I want to check your call records.

EMMA

Explain to me why I'd let you do that?

MURRAY

Don't play games.

                    EMMA
I'm not.

                    MURRAY
Do you work for the tabloids?

                    EMMA
No.

                    MURRAY
My ex-wife?

                    EMMA
No.

                    MURRAY
Then hand it over.

                    EMMA
No.
> *[Pause. MURRAY studies her for a moment—then hops over the bar and grabs his coat.]*

                    MURRAY
Nice meeting you.

                    EMMA
Jesus! What a fucking prima-donna!
> *[MURRAY stops.]*
You think just because you've published a few books you have some sort of divine right to my personal information?

                    MURRAY
No, I—

                    EMMA
What? Are you afraid somebody's gonna take your picture? Ask for your autograph? Oh my god! Somebody's asking for my autograph!

MURRAY

That isn't ... you don't understand—

EMMA

It's none of your fucking business who I called. Get over it.
　　[Pause.]

MURRAY

You're right.

EMMA

Fucking right, I'm right.

MURRAY

I'm sorry. I didn't mean to be an ass. It's just ... I don't know if you
read the tabloids, but my wife and I separated a few months ago,
right, and—

EMMA

She's pissed.

MURRAY

You could say that. She wants a lot of money. A lot. I didn't keel
over and give her every little thing she asked for, so now she's
playing it out in the press. Trying to pressure me. She knows how
bad publicity can affect book sales, and she figures I'll cave just to get
her to stop. But I don't care anymore. It doesn't matter. She's
actually hired a public relations firm and they're feeding the tabloids
all sorts of stories about women I'm supposedly fucking—

EMMA

Are you?

MURRAY

What?

EMMA

Fucking all these other women?

MURRAY

That isn't the point.

EMMA

What is the point?

MURRAY

The point is, the last thing I need is another story about me and
some—

EMMA

Some what?

MURRAY

—some beautiful, intelligent, young woman who, unfortunately—

EMMA

That's more like it.

MURRAY

I mean, you could be setting me up. Right? My wife could have paid
you, you know, to come here. To seduce me.

EMMA

You're really paranoid—aren't you? I mean, like really fucking crazy
paranoid?

MURRAY

Am I paranoid? Or are the bastards really out to get me?

EMMA

Let me ask you a question. A man approaches you in a restaurant. Is
he A: the waiter, B: a stalker, or C: a policeman about to arrest you
for accidentally visiting a porn site?

MURRAY

I have reason to be paranoid. If you ever meet my wife, you'll
understand. Ex-wife. Soon-to-be ex-wife.

                         EMMA
My husband thinks it's all trash.

                         MURRAY
Your husband?

                         EMMA
He thinks your wife's a bitter old hag.

                         MURRAY
Goddammit. You have a husband?

                         EMMA
A bitter old hag who doesn't want to give up the good life. And
you're just an innocent victim. A very rich, misunderstood, innocent
victim.

                         MURRAY
What do you think?

                         EMMA
I think there are two sides to every story.
     [Pause.]

                         MURRAY
How big is he? Your husband?

                         EMMA
How big?

                         MURRAY
Just out of curiosity. I mean, could he crush the life out of me with
just, you know, like his bare hands or something?
     [Pause.]
He could—couldn't he? He's like some giant, inhumanly strong,
radiation infected, mutant, super-powered sumo wrestler with giant
metal blades sticking out of his hands! Right? Something like that?

EMMA
No, you definitely have the size advantage.
        [Pause.]

MURRAY
I should go.

EMMA
Sit.

MURRAY
No, look, you're very pretty, but—

EMMA
You don't have any choice, Murray. It's Fate.

MURRAY
I don't believe in Fate.

EMMA
I do. I can see it where I used to see just random events. Take you,
for instance—Fate dropped me here, right in your lap.
        [She sits on his lap.]

MURRAY
Mmmm ... what for?

EMMA
Either to save you or destroy you.

MURRAY
I hope you're not here to destroy me.

EMMA
If it's fate, there's nothing either one of us can do to stop it.

MURRAY
That's quite the come on.

EMMA

Don't take my word for it. Ask Oedipus.

MURRAY

Oedipus?

EMMA

Uh-huh.

MURRAY

You're not my mother, are you?

EMMA

Do you want me to be?

MURRAY

Oh. You're a very naughty girl.

EMMA

I'm going to be completely honest with you.

MURRAY

Okay.

EMMA

I don't care that you're a celebrity, that you're famous, or rich, any of that. What you can do for me has nothing to do with your literary prowess.

MURRAY

And what can I do for you?

EMMA

My husband. He's obsessed with you.

MURRAY

We're back to the husband.

                           EMMA
He forces me to read your novels.

                           MURRAY
I'm so sorry.

                           EMMA
All of them.

                           MURRAY
It isn't too painful, I hope.

                           EMMA
They're a little too intellectual for my taste. I prefer a book that gets
right to the action, you know, the sex and violence. But I see the
appeal. There's something in them ... a freedom from inhibitions and
cultural judgments ... this devil-may-care, do anything attitude ...
let's just say I find them intriguing.

                           MURRAY
So you're not big on foreplay?

                           EMMA
It's a waste of fucking time.

                           MURRAY
Good to know.

                           EMMA
Anyway, you're all he ever talks about.

                           MURRAY
The husband?

                           EMMA
Yes.

MURRAY

We keep coming back to him.

EMMA

He has all these different theories—what you're planning to do with different characters and so on, who's going to end up with who, who you're going to kill off, you know, which characters are pretending to be something they're not, hiding their true identity, pursuing dark, hidden objectives—he goes on and on about it. Endlessly. I mean, he won't shut up. It's like a disease. You've infected his brain with this imaginary world of yours, and there's no room for anything else in there. Not his family. Not his friends. Not me. We can't even have a good fuck anymore without him forcing me to act out some scene from one of your books. He especially likes that last one.

MURRAY

Oh god.

EMMA

Yeah. The whole dungeon thing.

MURRAY

Right.

EMMA

Could you do me a favor? Could you write a love scene that doesn't involve the woman being whipped to a bloody pulp? Not that I didn't enjoy it as a change of pace, but—

MURRAY

Sorry. I was thinking of my wife when I wrote that. Ex-wife. My little revenge, you know.

EMMA

Talk to him. My husband.

MURRAY

I don't know if that's—

EMMA

Break this spell you have over him. Disillusion him, make him hate you, I don't care, whatever it takes.

MURRAY

I thought this was headed in an entirely different direction.

EMMA

Maybe it is.

MURRAY

Whiplash.

EMMA

Can your restore my husband to the world of the living? Slay the zombie?

MURRAY

I don't—

EMMA

If you can, I'd be very grateful.

MURRAY

Grateful?

EMMA

I might even offer a reward.

MURRAY

What kind of reward?

EMMA

Pick your poison.

* * *

SCENE II

[An apartment. EMMA enters, followed by MURRAY.]

EMMA

Harold!

HAROLD

[Offstage.]
Just a minute!

EMMA

I have a surprise for you!

HAROLD

I'm coming!

EMMA

Hurry up!

HAROLD

I'm coming! Don't rush me!

EMMA

There's someone here I want you to meet!
[Enter HAROLD, a harmless-looking man. He straightens his tie. EMMA laughs.]

HAROLD

What?

EMMA

What's this?

HAROLD

What do you mean?

EMMA

The suit! When did you—

19

HAROLD

I bought it. After you called.

EMMA

Oh for god's sake!

HAROLD

I didn't have anything to wear.

EMMA

You sound like a school-girl.

HAROLD

Shut up.

EMMA

What?

HAROLD

I said shut up.

EMMA

Don't talk to me like—

HAROLD

Shut your fucking mouth. Don't embarrass me in front of our new
friend.
        [Silence. EMMA exits to the bedroom.]
I'm sorry about that.

MURRAY

No …

HAROLD

We shouldn't involve you in our personal disputes.

MURRAY

It's all right.

HAROLD

No, it's embarrassing.

MURRAY

It's really none of my business.
*[HAROLD stares at MURRAY expectantly. He grins.
MURRAY offers his hand.]*
I'm Murray.
[They shake.]

HAROLD

I know who you are. When Emma called to tell me you were coming,
I couldn't believe my luck. I thought she was lying.

MURRAY

She called? That was you?

HAROLD

Oh! Would you like a drink?

MURRAY

Sure.

HAROLD

Whiskey sour?

MURRAY

My favorite.

HAROLD

I know. I know everything about you.

MURRAY

I hope not.

HAROLD

Emma! Two whiskey sours!

EMMA

[Offstage.]
Get them yourself!

HAROLD

Our guest would like a drink!

EMMA

Do I sound like I give a fuck?!

HAROLD

Don't embarrass me!

MURRAY

Really, it's all right ... I don't—

HAROLD

Get your lazy fucking whore ass out here right now or I swear to
God—
    [EMMA storms out of the bedroom and into the kitchen.]
I apologize for her behavior. She isn't usually like this.

MURRAY

No, don't apologize.

HAROLD

It's embarrassing.

MURRAY

Oh, I'm sure—

HAROLD

She does it to embarrass me.
    [To EMMA.]
Don't forget the cherries!

EMMA

[Offstage.]
I've got your fucking cherries!

HAROLD

You like cherries—right?

MURRAY

Yes. I do. I like cherries. Thank you.

HAROLD

I've read everything you've ever written.

MURRAY

I doubt that.

HAROLD

Everything. I even have copies of those short stories from your high school lit journal.

MURRAY

Did I have a high school lit journal?

HAROLD

Yes. You did. You wrote several stories.

MURRAY

Huh. I guess I'd forgotten.

HAROLD

It's not your best work. I mean, you were just a kid, how could it be, right? But there was already a seed, you know, a little seed, you were already starting to develop some of the themes you'd revisit in your early novels—love and cruelty, compassion and torture—

MURRAY

Are you a book critic or something?

HAROLD

No. I'm an accountant.

MURRAY

It's just, well, you sound like my agent's wet dream.
[Enter EMMA with two whiskey sours—one is full of cherries, one has none.]

EMMA

Here.

HAROLD

Wait.

EMMA

What?

HAROLD

Where's my cherry?

EMMA

I didn't give you one.

HAROLD

Why not?

EMMA

I didn't feel like it.

HAROLD

You didn't feel like it?

EMMA

No.

MURRAY

Here, you can have one of mine.

HAROLD

I don't want yours.

MURRAY

Really, it's not—

HAROLD

I want my lazy no-good whore of a wife to bring me my own goddamned fucking cherry and put it in my drink with her lazy little whore fingers before I slap the fuck out of her smirking lazy no-good slutwhore face.

EMMA

Nice. That's nice, Harold.
            [She exits to the kitchen and returns with a jar of cherries.
            She drops a handful into Harold's drink.]
Happy?

HAROLD

Yes. Thank you.

EMMA

Anything else I can do for you while I'm up?

HAROLD

You can take off that slutty dress.

EMMA

What?

HAROLD

I can see your tits. It's embarrassing.

EMMA

Bullshit.

HAROLD

The whole world can see your no-good fucking whore tits.

EMMA

Do my whore tits make you nervous, Harold?

HAROLD

Shut up.

EMMA

Don't tell me to—

HAROLD

Show a little class. Leave something to the imagination.
[EMMA storms into the bedroom.]

HAROLD

Where were we? Your early work?

MURRAY

Right.

HAROLD

You know, what fascinates me most, I think, is the through line of
your writing, as a whole, I mean, from those first short stories to this
last novel, there's a certain consistency that you just don't see from
most writers, a common thematic thread that binds everything
together, you know, deepens with each new narrative, adding
complimentary colors to the canvas, enriching everything that's come
before, illuminating the darkest corners ... documenting a whole new
world!

MURRAY

You really should consider a career in literary criticism.

HAROLD

I actually made a map, you know, of all the different locations in your
novels.

MURRAY

You ... you made a ...

HAROLD

A map.

MURRAY

Of all the—

HAROLD

Every country …

MURRAY

Every imaginary country?

HAROLD

Every stream and river …

MURRAY

Also imaginary …

HAROLD

But it all fit together! I charted every geographical location! Every landmark you ever described! Every little hill or valley! Every cave! And it was like a picture coming into view one pixel at a time! Like pieces of a puzzle, overlapping from one novel to the next until—before I knew it—you'd mapped out an entire world! Emma! Bring the map! There were a few little holes until this last novel, a few little grey areas, but you filled them in, everything connects now!

MURRAY

That's fascinating. Really. It is.

HAROLD

I thought for sure you'd mapped it out, that you had a map of your own somewhere, above your desk maybe, something you referred to—

MURRAY

Not exactly, no.

                         HAROLD

No?

                         MURRAY

I mean, I tried to keep a sort of vague map, in my head, you know,
very general, but not—

                         HAROLD

Maybe you could use it in your next book! My map! You wouldn't
have to give me credit or anything like that. Unless you want to. I
mean, I wouldn't turn it down. But you don't—

                         MURRAY

Well, look, I'd certainly be fascinated to see this map of yours—

                         HAROLD

Emma!

                         MURRAY

—But I'm afraid there won't be a next book.

                         HAROLD

What?

                         MURRAY

There won't be another book. I'm done.

                         HAROLD

Done?

                         MURRAY

Done. I think it's interesting that you say I've mapped out an entire
world—

                         HAROLD

Define *done*.

MURRAY

—that I've literally … because, well, that's what I've felt. I mean, I've felt there's nothing left to write, you know, there's nothing else to say.

HAROLD

You have things to say! Lots of things! Important things!

MURRAY

Not anymore. I've retired.

HAROLD

What? No!

MURRAY

There won't be any more books.

HAROLD

You … you can't be serious!

MURRAY

I sit in front of my computer and … nothing. There's nothing. I just stare at the screen. The cursor blinks at me like I'm some kind of idiot retard. Blink, blink, blink. Write something, stupid. Blink, blink, blink.

HAROLD

That's writer's block! It happens to every writer!

MURRAY

Not like this. I've had writer's block. This is … well, it's something different. Just silence. Like someone turned off the lights.

HAROLD

You could see a therapist! A therapist for writers! There must be such a thing! Right?

MURRAY

No, look, I'm sorry.

HAROLD

Don't say that!

MURRAY

It's why my wife left, actually. She'd gotten used to all the fanfare, you know, all the awards and parties, governor's balls, free gifts. She couldn't accept the fact it was all over.

HAROLD

This isn't true! You're lying! You're making this up!

MURRAY

Why would I do that?

HAROLD

Emma! She put you up to this! Didn't she?! She promised to fuck you if you broke my heart!

MURRAY

No, no, no, look … maybe I should just go.

HAROLD

I can't believe this is happening! This isn't happening!
[Enter EMMA with a rolled-up document.]

EMMA

You wanted this?

HAROLD

Yes! No!

MURRAY

Is that the map?

EMMA

Yup.

MURRAY

Could I see that, actually?

HAROLD

No!

EMMA

No? All that work and you're not even gonna let him see it?

HAROLD

This isn't real! You're not here! I can't hear you!

EMMA

You have no idea how many nights he's spent drooling over this
thing. How many years. Seriously. Every night. Sitting there with
his little colored pencils and his rulers and his stencil, hunched over,
like some grammar school kid doing his homework, pouring through
your books, popping a few pills, making notes in the margins, cup of
coffee, hunting for anything he might have missed, any geographic
reference, any clue you might have dropped, some breadcrumb,
anything he could convert into a solid number, a measurement. If you
wrote that some character travelled from point A to point B in, say,
two weeks, he'd actually calculate a predicted rate of travel and
extrapolate the distance so he could plot it on his map, then he'd
triangulate all known locations until he could pinpoint exactly how
everything fit together, until he could eliminate all other possibilities.
How many drafts did you make, Harold? Fifteen? Twenty? Thirty?
At first, I thought it was cute. He was so serious about the whole
thing. You should have seen him. He thought he was Lewis and
Clark, charting unexplored territory, but then he'd notice some little
mistake and tear the whole thing apart. Rip it to shreds. The map had
to be perfect. Flawless. It was like a religion. He wouldn't talk to
me. We stopped having sex. Sometimes he took sick days so he
could stay home and work on this monstrosity. I tried to distract him,
offer alternative activities. I'd strip down to nothing … whisper in his

EMMA (cont.)

ear ... dirty little thoughts ... you know ... suggestions ...
geometrical calculations of my own ... all the different ways that two
bodies can come together ... I'd brush my tits through his hair ... rub
myself against him like some bitch in heat ... nothing. No reaction.
He wouldn't even acknowledge my presence. Unless, of course, I'd
role-play, you know, pretend to be one of your goddamned characters,
then he'd throw himself on top of me like a sailor on shore leave, like
a preacher filled with the holy spirit—then I was his oracle at Delphi,
my body dispensing divine inspiration, but the moment I was me
again, the second I was Emma, he'd drift away like a ghost. Back to
the map. He didn't want any distractions from the map. And that's
all I was—a distraction. That's why I'm a whore, by the way—not
because I cheated or crawled into someone else's bed ... but because I
tried to lure him away from this!

HAROLD

That isn't true! That's not why! You know why!

EMMA

Oh Harold. You're so pathetic.

HAROLD

I told you to take off that slutty fucking no-good whoredress!

EMMA

You want me to take off this whoredress?

HAROLD

That's what I said!

EMMA

You want me to take it off?

HAROLD

How many times do I have to say it?

EMMA

All right! Fine!
    [She pulls the dress over her head.]
How's that?

HAROLD

Goddammit, woman!

EMMA

Is that better?

MURRAY

Maybe I should—

EMMA

Anything else you want me to take off?

HAROLD

My world is falling apart here!

EMMA

This? Or this?

HAROLD

Do you have to choose this particular moment to humiliate me?!

MURRAY

I can just—

HAROLD

In front of him, of all people!

EMMA

Maybe you'd like him to wear the dress, Harold! Maybe that's the
real problem!
    [HAROLD slaps her hard across the face.]

HAROLD

Leave him out of this!

MURRAY

Now, hold on!

HAROLD

This is none of your business!

MURRAY

I can't just stand here while you—

HAROLD

She's trying to turn you against me! Don't you see! That's what this is all about!

MURRAY

Are you all right?

HAROLD

She wants—

EMMA

I'm fine.

HAROLD

She wants to—

EMMA

That's it, Harold! That's it! That's the last straw!

HAROLD

I'll kill you! You stupid fucking whore!
    [HAROLD lunges at EMMA. MURRAY stops him.]

MURRAY

Calm down.

HAROLD

Get your hands off me! You came here to fuck my wife!
 [They fight. HAROLD falls and hits his head against a table.]

MURRAY

All right. Let's go.

EMMA

Wait ...

MURRAY

Let's get out of here.

EMMA

Hold on.

MURRAY

C'mon. Put some clothes on.

EMMA

Oh shit.

MURRAY

C'mon.

EMMA

Oh my god.

MURRAY

Get dressed. Hurry up. He'll be up any second.

EMMA

He isn't moving.

MURRAY

He hit his head.

                          EMMA
He's not …

                          MURRAY
I'm sure it's just—

                          EMMA
Is that blood?

                          MURRAY
Where?

                          EMMA
Oh my god.

                          MURRAY
There's blood?

                          EMMA
A lot.

                          MURRAY
Are you sure?

                          EMMA
His head.

                          MURRAY
He didn't hit it that hard. He barely—

                          EMMA
There's a lot of blood.

                          MURRAY
He barely tapped it.

                          EMMA
I can't tell if he's breathing—

MURRAY

He's not breathing?

EMMA

I can't tell.

MURRAY

Oh my god.

* * *

SCENE III

[A hotel room. MURRAY and EMMA enter quickly and shut the door behind them.]

MURRAY

Did anyone see us?

EMMA

No. I don't think so.

MURRAY

We shouldn't be here. Together, I mean. We shouldn't be together. It looks suspicious. What if someone sees?

EMMA

Who? Who would see?

MURRAY

I don't know.

EMMA

The police?

MURRAY

Maybe.

EMMA

No one saw.

MURRAY

How do you know?

EMMA

No one knows you were there.

MURRAY

If they find out, if they know I was there, they'll think I killed him.

EMMA

You did.

MURRAY

On purpose! They'll think I killed him on purpose—that we were having an affair, and he caught us together, and I killed him!

EMMA

Well, that is the most logical explanation—isn't it? That we were having an affair?

MURRAY

But we weren't! We weren't having an affair!

EMMA

No?

MURRAY

No!

EMMA

Are you sure?

MURRAY

What?

EMMA

Are you sure we weren't having an affair? Because I totally thought there was something going on.

MURRAY

Oh my god! I never should have gone with you! What was I thinking?!

EMMA

You were thinking about your reward. Duh.

                          MURRAY

My reward?

                          EMMA

Oh, c'mon.

                          MURRAY

I don't know what you're—

                          EMMA

Don't be stupid. I asked you to slay the zombie—

                          MURRAY

You don't think I intentionally—

                          EMMA

Intentionally or not, you kept your end of the bargain.
        [Taking off her dress.]
Now it's my turn.

                          MURRAY

Are you serious?
        [She continues to undress.]
You're going to sleep with me as a reward for accidentally murdering
your husband?

                          EMMA

Not as a reward. No.

                          MURRAY

A compensatory gift?

                          EMMA

I didn't want you to kill him, if that's what you're suggesting. I
expected a little subtlety. You are a writer after all. I thought you'd
play some sort of mind game. Get inside his head. Disillusion him
maybe. Not kill him.

MURRAY

A little subtlety?

EMMA

That's right.

MURRAY

I wasn't subtle enough?

EMMA

He's dead.

MURRAY

He attacked me!

EMMA

All right. Look. It doesn't matter. It's done. He's dead. I don't
want to argue.

MURRAY

All right. No arguing.

EMMA

It's in the past.

MURRAY

Forgotten.

EMMA

We should just move forward.

MURRAY

Moving forward.

EMMA

You should probably take off your clothes. That would be a good
first step.

MURRAY

You're serious about this? You're going to sleep with the man who just murdered your husband?

EMMA

It's not like I have any other option. Not really.

MURRAY

No? You didn't make the choice to come here? Who did, if not you? I mean, is there some stranger lurking in the shadows? Some mysterious figure manipulating events? Hiding just out of sight? Is someone twisting your arm?

EMMA

Yes.

MURRAY

What?

EMMA

Yes.

MURRAY

Yes?
    [She nods.]
Someone is? Someone's twisting your arm?
    [She nods.]
Who?
    [No response.]
Who is?
    [No response.]
Who's twisting your arm?
    [No response.]
C'mon.
    [No Response.]
I asked you a question.
    [No response.]

MURRAY (cont.)

Who is it?
   [No response.]
Is it my wife?
   [No response.]
Do you work for my wife?
   [No response.]
You do—don't you?
   [No response.]
Did she pay you to do this?
   [No response.]
To set this up? This whole thing?
   [No response.]
Oh my god! She did! You work for my wife! How could I be so
stupid! She somehow orchestrated this whole thing from behind the
scenes! Like some kind of spider! Weaving her little web! Sucking
me in! Knowing what would happen! Knowing I'd give her anything
to keep it out of the papers! Oh my god! That's assuming I don't go
to jail! I could actually go to jail! I mean, you could tell them
anything! You could tell them it was intentional! It would be my
word against yours! That fucking cunt! Whatever she's paying you,
I'll pay double! Triple! Whatever you want! Name your price!

EMMA

It's not your wife.

MURRAY

Oh. Good.
   [Pause.]
Who then?

EMMA

Fate.

MURRAY

Fate?

                         EMMA

I told you before—

                         MURRAY

Honey, I told *you* before—I don't believe in fate.

                         EMMA

Fate believes in you.

                         MURRAY

That's the stupidest fucking line I've ever heard in my life.

                         EMMA

I didn't write it.

                         MURRAY

You said it.

                         EMMA

I'm just the mouthpiece.

                         MURRAY

Then I'll only blame you for the bad delivery.

                         EMMA

Do you want me or not?

                         MURRAY

I haven't decided yet.

                         EMMA

Well, make up your mind, 'cause I don't have all day.

                         MURRAY

Here's the problem I'm having. I don't believe in Fate. Fate is a
manifestation of natural causes. That's it. It's not a conscious entity.
It has no plan. So ... if the hand of Fate isn't moving us across this
lovely little chess board ... and it isn't my wife's greedy little fingers

MURRAY (cont.)

moving the pieces … then who is it? Who's calling the shots?
Because there's some sort of agenda going on here. I'm not
completely blind. Someone in this room wants something from
someone else, and since I have no idea what that is, that thing that
someone wants, I'm starting to think I might be the victim here.

EMMA

You don't want anything?

MURRAY

No.

EMMA

Goodbye.

MURRAY

Hold on.

EMMA

Get out of my way!

MURRAY

Keep it down! They'll hear you!

EMMA

Get out of my way or I'll call the police!

MURRAY

Now, just one goddamned minute! Just one…. Let's not forget who
started all this! Okay?! I didn't track you down in some bar, or invite
you home, or ask you to "slay the zombie!" You dragged me into
this. I have a right to be suspicious.

EMMA

I'm not playing you, if that's what you're worried about.

MURRAY

Prove it.

EMMA

How?
> *[Pause.]*

MURRAY

I've done something illegal for you. What if I asked you to return the favor?

EMMA

You want me to do something illegal?

MURRAY

Maybe. What if I did?

EMMA

To even things up?

MURRAY

That way we've each got the goods, you know, on the other person. You won't stab me in the back if you know I can turn around and do the same to you.
> *[Pause.]*

EMMA

I can't really refuse, can I? I mean, it's Fate, right?

MURRAY

Right.
> *[Pause.]*

EMMA

Were you serious? What you told Harold before? About retiring?

MURRAY

Yeah, it's all true. I'm tapped out. My wife thinks I'm doing it just to aggravate her. She wants a ridiculous amount of money—which is completely unrealistic if I stop writing. Her lawyer says it's a choice to stop writing.

EMMA

Isn't it?

MURRAY

No.

EMMA

What is it then? If not a choice?

MURRAY

I don't know.

EMMA

Fate?

MURRAY

No. Not Fate.

EMMA

What then?

* * *

SCENE IV

*[MURRAY'S former home. There is a knock. SARAH
enters from the kitchen. She wears a bathrobe. Her hair is up
in a towel. She opens the front door.]*

SARAH

Can I help you?

EMMA

Yes, I'm from Goldberg & McCann.

SARAH

What do you want?

EMMA

I'm supposed to have you sign a few papers.

SARAH

A few papers?

EMMA

That's right.

SARAH

I thought we handled that this morning. At the office.

EMMA

No, we missed a few.

SARAH

We missed a few?

EMMA

Yes.

SARAH

We just missed them? Are you people completely incompetent?

I mean, there's always something—isn't there? You don't ever get
things right the first time. I wonder why that is? You don't think it
might have anything to do with the outrageous fees you're charging
me to fix the things you didn't get right the first time—do you? You
couldn't possibly be running up the tab?

Look, I'm just a legal assistant.

Are you charging me for this visit? Is this on the clock?

I'm just following instructions. You can call and check if you'd like.
[Pause.]

No. I believe you. Come in.

Thank you.
[EMMA enters.]

We can go over everything at the coffee table.

This is a lovely house.
[Pause.]
Very tasteful. What you've done with it.

That's what I go for. Tasteful.

                         EMMA

I didn't mean to offend you.

                         SARAH

I'm not offended.

                         EMMA

It was a compliment.

                         SARAH

That's how I took it.
        [Pause.]
Can we get on with this? You may not think it, but I do have a life.

                         EMMA

Sorry. Just let me get set up here.
        [EMMA opens her briefcase and pulls out a stack of papers.]
I've always wanted a house like this.
        [Pause.]
With the trees, you know. And the windows.
        [Pause.]
You have beautiful windows.
        [Pause.]
How much does a place like this sell for?

                         SARAH

I have no idea.

                         EMMA

You must have some.

                         SARAH

No.

                         EMMA

I mean, it must be expensive.

SARAH

Well, yes, it's expensive. Of course it's expensive. That's a given. I mean, look at the neighborhood. But my husband handles all the bills. All right? Used to. Used to handle. Before he left. So I don't know any of the details. How much the fucking house was. Anything like that.

EMMA

I'm sorry. I didn't mean—

SARAH

No, it's all right.
    [Pause.]

EMMA

He's a writer—isn't he? Your husband?

SARAH

Unfortunately.

EMMA

Did he ever write about you?

SARAH

It's not as romantic as you might think.

EMMA

No? I think it must be wonderful. To be immortalized like that.

SARAH

Sure. It was flattering at first. I was the love interest back then, the heroine, you know, just dripping sexuality, inspiring armies with my charms, seducing heroes with a look. It was good for the ego, I'll say that much. All my friends were terribly jealous. But even then, I had this dark side. In his books, I mean. Not in real life. He always gave me a selfish streak or some petty score to settle, some obsession that compromised his hero in some way. I thought he was just trying to make things more interesting, you know, unpredictable, lifelike, but

SARAH (cont.)

then I started noticing little bits of myself in the villains, the really evil characters, right, the kind that need a stake through the heart to put them out of their misery. He denied it, of course. Said I was being paranoid. But there were certain things I'd say, you know, certain conversations we'd had that he'd repeat almost word for word. It was so obvious. The heroines no longer resembled me at all. They were young and pretty and innocent, and he'd chase after them, just like he did in real life, and I was this aging, bitter hag out to destroy him, determined to make his life as miserable and pathetic as my own. My only consolation is that after the divorce, I'll get a cut of book royalties. That's what we're asking. I think it's only fair, don't you? That every time someone realizes what a contemptible cunt I am, at least I'll make a few dollars?

EMMA

Oh no.

SARAH

What?

EMMA

Shit.

SARAH

What's wrong?

EMMA

I forgot my list. My list of everything you've already signed.

SARAH

Maybe we should just do this tomorrow.

EMMA

No! Wait! I'm gonna be in so much trouble!

SARAH

That's really not my problem.

EMMA

Couldn't I just take a quick peek at your copies?

SARAH

My copies?

EMMA

Just a quick peek.

SARAH

Why would you need my copies?

EMMA

To mark off what you've already signed. Then I can have you sign
the others and get out of your hair. You won't have to waste any time
tomorrow, and I don't make a bad impression on the partners.
Everybody wins.
   [Pause.]
Please?
   [Pause.]

SARAH

All right. Fine. But I'm only doing this to help you out.
   [SARAH exits. She returns with a handful of papers.]
I think that's everything.

EMMA

Thank you so much. I really appreciate this.
   [EMMA studies the papers. SARAH studies EMMA.]

SARAH

I don't think I've seen you over there.

EMMA

At the office?

SARAH

That's right. Are you new?

                    EMMA
No.

                    SARAH
No?

                    EMMA
No. I've been around.
    [Pause.]

                    SARAH
I wonder why I haven't seen you.

                    EMMA
Couldn't say.
    [Pause.]
I mean, I do run a lot of errands.
    [Pause.]
I'm out of the office a lot.
    [Pause.]
Quite a bit, actually.

                    SARAH
Who hired you?

                    EMMA
What?

                    SARAH
Who hired you?

                    EMMA
Who hired me?

                    SARAH
That's right. Was it Joe or Mike?

EMMA

I don't see what this has to do with—

SARAH

Answer the question.

EMMA

I'm not—

SARAH

Which one?

EMMA

Neither.

SARAH

Who then?

EMMA

Dan.

SARAH

That's right. Dan does most of the hiring.

EMMA

So I pass?

SARAH

What?

EMMA

This little quiz.
    [Pause.]

SARAH

Sorry. I may be a little paranoid. I've never gone through a divorce before. I don't really trust anyone right now. There's a lot of money involved, you know.

[*Pause.*]

EMMA

Could I ask a small favor?

SARAH

Of course.

EMMA

My throat's bothering me and I have this tea that helps. I've got a teabag in my briefcase. Could I possibly …

SARAH

You want to make a cup?

EMMA

If you don't mind.

SARAH

No. Go ahead.

EMMA

Thank you. It really helps.

SARAH

Cups are in the kitchen.
        [*SARAH points. EMMA exits with her teabags.*]
There's a button for hot water. On the refrigerator.

EMMA

Oh, one of the fancy kinds!

SARAH

Yes. The fancy kinds.

EMMA

May I borrow some honey?

SARAH

Knock yourself out. I can't eat the stuff. I used to get so mad at Murray for even having it in the house.

EMMA

Why?

SARAH

I have terrible food allergies. Honey makes my throat swell up. I almost died once. Didn't even know I'd had any.

EMMA

That's awful!
        [EMMA returns with two cups of tea.]
I made one for you too.

SARAH

I don't want any.

EMMA

It's delicious.

SARAH

No.

EMMA

You have to try.

SARAH

I don't like tea.

EMMA

It's really good. Smell.

SARAH

It does smell good.

EMMA

I can't get through the day without it. I'm completely addicted.

SARAH

[Takes a sip.]
It's sweet.

EMMA

Licorice. It's a dessert tea.

SARAH

Where do you buy it?

EMMA

Oh, any store.

SARAH

[Takes another sip.]
Is the paperwork ready?

EMMA

Just about. Yes.

SARAH

I apologize if I was short with you earlier.

EMMA

No. Not at all.

SARAH

It's just difficult, you know.

EMMA

I'm sure.

SARAH

Constantly having to watch my back. Make sure someone doesn't take advantage. I mean, all this money. It's such a headache.

EMMA

Well, it'll all be over soon.

SARAH

I hope so.

EMMA

You can move on.

SARAH

Yes. I plan on taking a long trip.

EMMA

Do you?

SARAH

As far away from here as possible.
[She clears her throat.]
Dubai maybe. I've never been to Dubai.
[She clears her throat again.]

EMMA

What's wrong?

SARAH

Nothing. My throat.
[Again, she clears her throat.]

EMMA

Have a sip of tea.
[She does.]
I hear Dubai's wonderful. The nightlife. Of course, I could never afford it myself. Not on my salary. It's never been an option, you know, not right now, but I hope someday—
[Again, SARAH clears her throat.]
Are you sure you're all right?

                          SARAH

Did you put honey in this tea?

                          EMMA

What?

                          SARAH

Honey! Is there honey in my tea?!

                          EMMA

No.

                          SARAH

Are you sure? It's sweet!
          [Clears her throat.]

                          EMMA

Licorice. It's naturally—

                          SARAH

But there's honey in yours?!

                          EMMA

Yes.

                          SARAH

Taste it!

                          EMMA

What?

                          SARAH

Taste it! Taste yours! Your tea!
          [SARAH clears her throat. EMMA takes a sip of tea.]
Do you taste honey?

                          EMMA

No, I … I don't—

SARAH

You stupid bitch! You gave me the wrong cup!

EMMA

Did I?

SARAH

Are you trying to kill me?!

EMMA

I'm so sorry. I—
                [SARAH clears her throat.]

SARAH
                [She is having difficulty speaking now.]
Call the hospital!

EMMA

What?

SARAH

The hospital! Call the hospital! A doctor!

EMMA

I can't understand you.

SARAH

A doctor! Call a doctor! Do it now!
                [SARAH clears her throat.]

EMMA

Maybe you could write it down.

SARAH
                [Straining to speak, barely audible.]
What?!

EMMA

Write it down. I can't understand what you're saying.

[SARAH clutches her throat now. She cannot breathe.]

* * *

SCENE V

[A hotel room.]

MURRAY

You weren't supposed to kill her!

EMMA

It just happened.

MURRAY

It just happened?!

EMMA

[Shrugs.]
Fate.

MURRAY

Oh my god!

EMMA

Look—

MURRAY

All I wanted was the paperwork! To know what they were going to file! What their strategy was!

EMMA

It was an accident. The honey was there. I put it in my drink. Somehow I switched the cups. It was just a freak thing. Don't get all worked up.

MURRAY

Don't get all worked up?! There's no possible way anyone could believe this was an accident! I killed your husband, you killed my wife! Within twenty-four hours! That doesn't just happen! Those are not random events! It's too convenient! We're going to jail!

EMMA

Calm down.

MURRAY

We have to split up. We can't be seen together.

EMMA

No one knows I was there.
[There is a knock at the door.]

MURRAY

What was that?
[Pause.]
Was that our door?

EMMA

Should I answer?

MURRAY

No. Did someone follow you?
[EMMA shrugs.]
Maybe they'll go away.
[Another knock.]
It's probably just the wrong room.
[Another knock, more insistent.]

EMMA

I'll get it.

MURRAY

Wait! What are you—
[Another knock, very loud.]

EMMA

He's gonna have the whole floor's attention if he keeps knocking like that! You want the whole floor's attention?

MURRAY

No. But—

[EMMA opens the door. HAROLD enters.]

HAROLD

Hello.

[Silence.]

MURRAY

What's going on?

[No answer.]

You're ... you're not dead.

HAROLD

Very observant. He's got his thinking cap on now.

MURRAY

So you ... the hand ... the hand that was moving all the ... it was you ... all the time ... the little pieces ... you and ... the two of ...

HAROLD

Calm down and try to speak in complete sentences.

[HAROLD produces a digital tape recorder and hits "play."]

MURRAY'S RECORDED VOICE

I've done something illegal for you. What if I asked you to return the favor?

EMMA'S RECORDED VOICE

You want me to do something illegal?

MURRAY'S RECORDED VOICE

Maybe. What if I did?

EMMA'S RECORDED VOICE

To even things up?

MURRAY'S RECORDED VOICE

That way we've each got the goods, you know, on the other person. You won't stab me in the back if you know I can turn around and do the same to you.

[HAROLD stops the tape player.]

MURRAY

You bugged the room? That isn't legal. You can't use that in court.

HAROLD

There are all kinds of legal ways I could have made that tape.

MURRAY

What do you want?

HAROLD

The rights to all your books.

MURRAY

My books?

HAROLD

All of them. I want you to walk away, disappear, go off into the woods and, I don't know, pull a J. D. Salinger, become a monk, whatever you want, I don't care, just leave me the books, the royalties, all the rights. No one will question it. Writers are crazy, everybody knows that.

MURRAY

So you really are a fan then?

HAROLD

You don't even know what you've written. What it is.

EMMA

Don't get all weird on us, Harold. Let's focus on the task at hand.

MURRAY

What about her?

HAROLD

Emma?

MURRAY

Does she get a cut?

HAROLD

Sure. She's my wife.

MURRAY

How much?

HAROLD

Half.

MURRAY

Half?

HAROLD

That's right.

MURRAY

Are you serious?

HAROLD

Sure. She's been a good little girl.

MURRAY

Isn't she sort of implicated in this too? I mean, couldn't I tell the police the two of you planned this whole—

HAROLD

You're gonna tell the truth? Go on. I dare you. No one would believe a word. I have a tape of you plotting your wife's murder.

MURRAY

That's taken completely out of context.

HAROLD

Your fingerprints are all over the crime scene.

MURRAY

I lived there.

HAROLD

Exactly. You had access. You had motive. I'm not stupid, Murray.
Okay? I'm not an idiot. I wouldn't have done this if I hadn't
considered every possible move you might make, what I'd do if you
did this or that, there are a multitude of scenarios playing out in my
head. If we're locked in a game of crazy chess, I'm ten moves ahead.
Your king is trapped, my queen's breathing down his neck, my
knight's running him down like a pig, and my bishop's bashing his
fucking brains in all over the chess board. There's no way out. I
didn't leave anything to chance. Nothing. Okay? We documented
the whole thing, from the beginning, planted evidence, well, most of it
you practically gift-wrapped, actually. I should thank you. You made
things not only very easy but also kind of entertaining in a goofy,
bumbling, Three Stooges sort of way. It was like a little in-flight
movie on our way to your money, where we'll be landing in just a few
minutes. If you were to actually tell the truth, I mean, first of all, I'm
not sure you even know what that is, the truth, but if you were to
attempt to tell it, you would sound so unbelievably batshit crazy, no
one would believe a single fucking word. No one. Not your closest
friend. Not your mommy. Sign everything over to me. Everything.
I'll lock the evidence up someplace safe. No one will ever see it.
You can live out the rest of your angst-ridden, tortured writer's
existence, signing autographs and banging starstruck fans at
conventions and, who knows, maybe you could even write another
book, you know, start over, new characters, new world. Completely
unwritten. Brand new adventure. That wouldn't be so bad—would
it? I mean, don't you kind of miss the old days? Be honest. Before
you had it made? Back when everything was still an adventure?
Don't you miss that? Just a little bit?

MURRAY

I do, actually. Yes.

HAROLD

Of course you do! You're only human! That's what human beings
long for! A new challenge! Right? A new obstacle to overcome!
That's what we're giving you! Okay? That's our little gift to you!

EMMA

The papers are ready to sign by the way. We took the liberty of
having them drawn up. I hope you don't mind.

HAROLD

Shut up.

EMMA

What?

HAROLD

Let me handle this.

EMMA

Don't tell me to—

HAROLD

Shut the fuck up. I was talking.

EMMA

You were talking?

HAROLD

Shut your no-good slutwhore mouth.

EMMA

Goddammit, Harold.

HAROLD

This doesn't make up for what you've done! We're not even! I can call you any fucking name I want! Whore! Bitch! Slut!

MURRAY

This part wasn't an act then? All the no-good whore tits stuff?

HAROLD

It's none of your goddamned—
   [MURRAY punches HAROLD in the face.]
What the hell was that?! I have your balls in a deathgrip, mister! Do you really want to piss me off?!

MURRAY

Give me the tape.

HAROLD

No. I have other—
   [MURRAY lunges for the tape recorder. They fight.]
You want to help me out here?!

EMMA

Sorry. Busy.
   [She picks up a magazine. They fight.]

HAROLD

I'm sorry I yelled at you! Help me!

EMMA

I don't do violence. You boys will have to handle that.
   [MURRAY punches HAROLD in the face.]

HAROLD

Goddammit!
   [HAROLD pulls a knife.]
I'm not completely defenseless. Okay? You're going to sign those papers. You don't have any choice. All I have to do is make one call, one call, okay, and you go to jail forever.

MURRAY

Oh, that sounds so trite.

HAROLD

Fuck you. I don't care what it sounds like. And you, missy, you just gave up your half. Okay? Fuck you both.

EMMA

I'm sorry? What was that?

HAROLD

You heard me. I don't need you.

EMMA

You'd better come back to reality. Real quick.

HAROLD

Fucking whore.

EMMA

Don't do it, Harold. This is a numbers game. This game we're playing. Whoever has the most numbers wins.

HAROLD

What the fuck is that supposed to mean?

EMMA

It means I'm the swing vote. You don't wanna fuck with me.

HAROLD

I will slice you both up and flush you down the fucking toilet if I have to! Do you understand?! No one is gonna turn this around on me!

MURRAY

[To EMMA.]
What do you think? You feel safer with this lunatic or with me?

HAROLD

Shut up!

EMMA

He makes a good point, Harold. You're gonna slice me up? That
doesn't make a girl feel safe.

HAROLD

You don't seriously think—

EMMA

I mean, why do you even say shit like that?

HAROLD

You know why!
            [Pause.]
All right. Look. I'll cut you back in. Okay? You can have fifteen
percent.

EMMA

            [Laughs.]
Fifteen percent?

HAROLD

Twenty.

EMMA

Twenty-five.

HAROLD

Fine. Twenty-five.

EMMA

Thirty.

HAROLD

You just said—

EMMA

Thirty-five. Hell, why not fifty? It was fifty a few minutes ago.

HAROLD

All right. Fine. Fine. Fifty. Okay?

EMMA

You're not going to give me anything.

HAROLD

Sure I am.

EMMA

You never were. After we're done with him, you're gonna leave me by the side of the road somewhere with that knife through my fucking heart.

HAROLD

Emma ... you know this guy, okay, you know the power he has to ... to pull ... I mean, he's a writer, okay, he comes up with shit like this for a living. He's putting ideas in your head. Manipulating you.

EMMA

There's nobody in my head but me.

HAROLD

Right. Just you and all the other crazy bitches in there.

EMMA

Okay. That's it. You just fucked yourself.

HAROLD

[To MURRAY.]

All right, look, you don't have to give us the whole thing. Okay? Not every book, not the whole collection, just ... just half. That's fair. We take half, you take half. Your wife was going to take half anyway. Right? I mean, you're not really losing anything.

MURRAY

Is that why you killed her? For my books?

HAROLD

Half. It's fair. A fair business transaction. Everybody's happy. We walk away. It's like this never happened.

EMMA

Who's fifty am I splitting?

HAROLD

What?

EMMA

I'm just trying to get a better understanding, you know, where I fit into this deal.

HAROLD

You can split with me. My half. Okay? Everybody happy?

EMMA

So that leaves me with …

HAROLD

Half of fifty. Twenty-five percent.

EMMA

[To MURRAY.]
Do you have a counter-offer.

HAROLD

What?

MURRAY

Half. Straight up.

HAROLD

What do you mean counter offer?

                          EMMA
Half for me, half for you?

                          MURRAY
Nothing for him.

                          HAROLD
Nothing for me? Nothing? Are you fucking crazy?!
          [Pause.]
I have a knife!
          [Pause.]
One million dollars. Okay? One million. That's nothing to you.
You won't even know it's gone.

                          MURRAY
          [To EMMA.]
Lock the door.
          [She does.]

                          HAROLD
Do you see this knife in my hand?! Are you blind?! I'm not the
victim here! Okay? You're the victim!
          *[HAROLD makes a rush for the door. MURRAY tackles him
          and wrestles the knife away.]*

                          MURRAY
Here.
          *[MURRAY tosses the knife to EMMA and throws HAROLD on
          the bed.]*

                          HAROLD
No! Wait! Wait! You don't understand! You don't know what
she—
          *[MURRAY presses a pillow over HAROLD'S face. As he
          suffocates, HAROLD struggles frantically.]*

                          * * *

EPILOGUE

[A beach. EMMA and MURRAY sip cocktails and watch a beautiful sunset.]

MURRAY

We can never go back.

EMMA

You're so fucking paranoid.

MURRAY

We're wanted for murder in a world where every credit card purchase is tracked, your cell phone transmits your exact global position, and every email you send is saved on dozens of computers before it reaches its final destination. We were lucky to get out of the country.

EMMA

Especially with all that money.

MURRAY

Yes. That was a risk.

EMMA

But it paid off—didn't it?

MURRAY

It did.

EMMA

I told you.

MURRAY

You told me.

EMMA

I've always wanted to see the world.

> MURRAY

Well, now's your chance.

> EMMA

We could go to Dubai. I hear it's lovely.

> MURRAY

[Laughs.]
It really isn't fair—is it?

> EMMA

What?

> MURRAY

We should be in jail.

> EMMA

We really should.

> MURRAY

I mean, I should be sharing a bunk with some giant, hulking, tattooed inmate. Right?

> EMMA

You'd be sharing more than that, I imagine.

> MURRAY

Oh no. Not by choice.

> EMMA

You'd resist?

> MURRAY

I think so. Yes. Wouldn't you?

> EMMA

You haven't learned to trust Fate yet?

MURRAY

She's treated me all right. So far.

EMMA

Your bunkmate might be very beautiful. On the inside, I mean. He could be everything you've ever wanted. Your soulmate.

MURRAY

I suppose you'd be off seducing the guards.

EMMA

Of course. For special treatment. You know. Cigarettes. Or an extra scoop of applesauce.
            [Pause. He studies her.]

MURRAY

I had an idea. For a new novel. Did I tell you?

EMMA

No. Harold would be thrilled.

MURRAY

It starts with two strangers in a dark, half-lit bar.

EMMA

Isn't that kind of stereotypical.

MURRAY

It all depends on where you go from there. I have a few ideas.

EMMA

Are you going to immortalize me?

MURRAY

Maybe. Maybe I will.

EMMA

But how?

MURRAY

What do you mean?

EMMA

How can you write me—when you don't know me at all?

MURRAY

I think I may have picked up a few clues to your character.

EMMA

Think so?

MURRAY

Not to suggest that you're not still a bit of an enigma, but, I mean, that's what I do. I'm a writer. I watch people.
    [EMMA laughs.]

EMMA

You really don't remember—do you?

MURRAY

Remember what?

EMMA

Me.

MURRAY

You?

EMMA

Yes.

MURRAY

I don't understand.

EMMA

I thought you knew. In the bar. I thought you realized.

MURRAY

Realized what?

EMMA

We've met before.

MURRAY

Have we?

EMMA

Yes.

MURRAY

Before the bar?

EMMA

Before everything. Years ago.

MURRAY

I'm pretty sure I'd remember.

EMMA

I was a little more reserved back then. Kind of mousy. We went to a convention. Some sort of expo or something. You were signing books.

MURRAY

Did I sign something for you?

EMMA

You did more than that.

MURRAY

Did I? I don't remember.

EMMA

I'm sure there were lots of girls at lots of conventions.

MURRAY

There were a few. The English teachers love me, especially the
young ones, you know, with their thesis novels, fresh out of college
… you weren't an English teacher?

EMMA

No. Harold dragged me. I didn't want to go. Not my thing, you
know. But there was some lecture you were giving. You seemed so
sure of yourself … up there on the stage … so full of knowledge and
confidence … nothing like Harold … I was just drawn to you …
sucked into your gravitational pull … into your web … like a fly.
    [Pause.]
It was the first time I'd ever cheated.

MURRAY

Sorry about that.

EMMA

I couldn't look Harold in the eye. He knew right away what I'd
done—didn't know with who, not then, not right away, I couldn't just
tell him. I mean, you were his hero, you know, his reason for
crawling out of bed in the morning. When I finally did, tell him,
that's when he started his ridiculous map. That stupid map. That
goddamned fucking no-good map. That night, with you, at the
convention. That's what set everything in motion. Weird, huh?

MURRAY

Weird.

EMMA

Probably Fate.

MURRAY

Fate. For sure.

EMMA

And now, here we are, sipping cocktails on the beach and living
happily ever after.

MURRAY

"I am the child of Fortune, the giver of good, and I shall not be shamed. She is my mother; my sisters are the Seasons; my rising and my falling match with theirs."

EMMA

Is that something you wrote?

MURRAY

No. I'm not that good. It's *Oedipus*, actually.
        [Pause.]

EMMA

He wrote to you once. Did you know that?

MURRAY

Oedipus?

EMMA

Harold. You wrote back.

MURRAY

Did I? I don't usually do that.

EMMA

No?

MURRAY

No. Not usually.
        [Pause.]
It's strange that I would.
        [Pause.]
I mean, it isn't the norm.
        [Pause.]
What did I say?

EMMA

I don't remember.

MURRAY

No idea?

EMMA

Something short. You didn't take much time.

MURRAY

I get a lot of letters. It isn't humanly possible, you know, to read
them all, much less make some sort of thoughtful reply. Not to every
one.

EMMA

He liked it well enough. He had it framed.

MURRAY

Did he?

EMMA

He put it on the wall, in his office. On the rare occasion we'd actually
have someone over, he'd drag them in there, first thing, you know,
force them to admire whatever few words you'd scribbled out. It's
strange that he didn't show you. Some little thing you said, but taken
as if it was the word of God.

MURRAY

He kept it? Even after he knew? About us?
        [She nods.]
You don't remember what I wrote?

EMMA

I really don't.

MURRAY

Wouldn't it be strange if it was prophetic in some way? Looking
back, I mean? Reading it now?

EMMA

Yes. That would be strange.

MURRAY

A message from the past. From my own hand.
    [Pause.]
It's still there?

EMMA

Yes.
    [Pause.]

MURRAY

We could sneak back into the country.

EMMA

I thought we couldn't go back?

MURRAY

Just take a quick peek, you know. I'm curious.

EMMA

You know what they say. About curiosity.
    [Pause.]
Care for a swim?

MURRAY

I'm not big on water.

EMMA

No?

MURRAY

No. Harold would know that.

EMMA

I'm sure he would.

MURRAY

I almost drowned once.

EMMA

Did you?

MURRAY

When I was a kid. Haven't been in the water since.

EMMA

We'll just splash around.

MURRAY

I didn't bring a suit.

EMMA

Neither did I.
        [She slips out of her dress.]

MURRAY

Oh. You're such a naughty girl.

EMMA

I know.
        [He does not move.]
What's the matter? Aren't you coming?
        [Pause.]
Don't you trust me?
        [Pause. EMMA laughs.]

MURRAY

What's so funny?

EMMA

Oh my god! You look so serious! You should see your face! Like
you think I'm about to drown you or something!
        [She continues to undress.]

MURRAY

What if you are? What if Fate sent you here to destroy me?

EMMA

Then there's nothing either one of us can do to stop it.
        [She stands naked before him.]
Are you coming?
        [Pause.]

MURRAY

What if someone sees?

EMMA

Who? Who would see?
        [Pause. He does not move.]

* * *

2074489R10044

Printed in Great Britain
by Amazon.co.uk, Ltd.,
Marston Gate.